LORDS OF THE REMNANT

MICHAEL KINGSWOOD

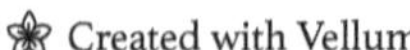 Created with Vellum

CONTENTS

ABOUT THIS BOOK

An infantryman, certain resistance is futile, nevertheless deploys with his unit to fight against an alien invasion.

Lords of the Remnant is a 3,800 word military science fiction short story.

~

Enjoy the book! After you're done, please come to Michael's website and sign up for his mailing list at michaelkingswood.com/newsletter-signup/. Guaranteed to be spam free, he uses it to announce new releases and special promotions for his fans.

LORDS OF THE REMNANT

They came at dawn, a streaming mass of bodies falling from the sky. As with everything else about them, this method of attack took us completely by surprise, and we had no immediate defense against it.

It was as though we were half a step behind them each time we met.

When the Centauri colony reported contact with craft of unknown origin, the people living in the various settlements in the Sol system were amazed, excited, filled with joy.

We were no longer alone! It was real, and undeniable.

Two weeks later, when the next transmission from Centauri brought news of the opening of hostilities, that feeling of euphoria changed to one of dread.

Mankind had stopped warring with itself centuries ago. With the exception of certain outlaw elements, the average person had no concept of war, or how to fight one. Yes, there were old warships drydocked in a station orbiting at the trans-lunar La-Grange point, near the James Webb historical site, but it had been decades since the reserve units charged with their maintenance had even powered them up.

All at once, though, those relics of man's warlike past became the Sol system's only hope of defense, and every available resource was put to making the small armada ready for action. But as further transmissions arrived from Centauri, we all began to realize that thirty ships, crewed by people with no experience in battle, would be of little use against the invaders if they came to Sol next.

And so Congress voted to build planetary defense grids on Earth, Mars, Luna, Europa, and Titan. The theory was that if we built large automated weapons arrays, the planets would be impregnable against any vessels that managed to make it past our small battle fleet.

The problem was time.

Centauri was about four light years away. At our best cruising speeds, it was a trip of about ten earth years, and that was damn little time to build the kinds of systems the plans called for.

But the continuing transmissions from Centauri provided all the motivation we needed. Pictures of the aliens' relentless advance, and our kinsmen's inevitable defeat, spurred every industry to put aside everything except war preparations.

When, two years after the first one, the final transmission from Centauri came through, a static-laced image of a man with hopeless, yet undefeated eyes bidding farewell to the rest of us, we figured we had at a minimum another five or six years to prepare. The aliens would want to take time to lick their wounds, consolidate their holdings, before they moved on, wouldn't they?

They arrived a month later.

How they managed it, even our greatest scientists could not explain. It meant they'd travelled so close to the speed of light that there was no point in measuring the difference. Assuming they'd left Centauri immediately after the final battle. If they'd lingered at all to regroup...well, that meant the impossible: they'd travelled faster than light to reach Sol, and that could not be.

Could it?

Titan and Europa were overrun almost immediately. Their defense grids were only just being started, and their small populations were ill-prepared to fight off the aliens' assault.

Our small armada met the alien fleet between Mars and Jupiter. They put up a good struggle, but in the end they were outnumbered and outgunned. With our fleet gone, the aliens advanced on the Mars colonies.

They held out a lot longer. Many of us on Earth and Luna wanted to send forces to assist the colonies in resisting the attack. We thought that if we joined humanity's forces in one place, we had a decent chance of beating them back.

But "wiser" heads prevailed, and the powers that be determined to instead focus on building up the Terran defense grid. In the year it took for Mars to fall, we built an impressive array of particle beam cannons, EMP transmitters, orbital minefields, and numerous other devices designed to ward off the alien fleet.

But when it came to be our turn, the invaders did not oblige us. Their fleet stood off, well beyond Luna's orbit, and did nothing.

Or so we thought.

Late last night, satellite observation posts detected small bursts of energy from the alien ships.

At first, we didn't know what was going on. But then, just a couple hours ago, low earth orbit weather analysis satellites detected thousands upon thousands of small objects approaching re-entry interface. Our defense grid, designed to target and take out the aliens' large battleships, never even noticed the multitude of man-sized craft until it was too late.

The civil defense sirens went off at five o'clock local time, rousing the populace, those who'd been able to sleep at all, in time to see the last of the plasma trails burn out as the aliens completed re-entry and plunged through the air toward the ground.

I had the midwatch in the civil defense station on the south side of town. When the report came in, I suggested we not sound the sirens at all. Better to not panic people.

After all, wouldn't dying in your sleep be preferable to living in desperate fear for a few hours before the end?

Of course, that was easy for me to say, as my Lieutenant kindly pointed out. The schmuck actually gave a speech about how we were going to beat these alien bastards back. We were going to whip their asses, you understand.

I managed to suppress a sarcastic reply, but I'm sure he saw my smirk. But what was we he going to do, write me up? We needed every swinging dick who could hold a rifle out in the field, and he knew it.

So that's how I found myself at the outskirts of the forest southeast of town, watching the tens of thousands of tiny black specks that I knew were alien shock troops grow larger and larger in the sky. I looked left and right at the other guys in my platoon and wondered, for the hundredth time, what the hell we were doing.

There were maybe a couple hundred of us, total. There was no way we'd be able to hold them on our own. Headquarters had promised help was on the way as soon as it could get here from the staging area a hundred clicks west, but the aliens were dropping in all over the world, from what I could tell.

It would be way past lucky if they didn't drop on the staging area as well.

Then there was no time to think about it. The first of the invading troopers flared, metallic wings similar to a butterfly's extending from its metallic re-entry suit, and settled onto the ground maybe half a kilometer ahead of our lines.

No one had to give the order to fire. A hundred Particle Rifles, smaller cousins of the particle beam cannons in orbit around the Earth, fired nearly in unison, and the first alien disappeared in a super-heated fireball.

But a second landed. Then a third. A fifth. A twentieth. A hundredth.

We dispatched the first hundred or so easily enough. They landed far enough apart that we were able to concentrate our fire to take them out quickly. But after that, they began landing in groups of ten or twenty, and it was all we could do to hold our ground. The invaders fell by the dozen as we fell back, but for every one that fell, ten landed behind it as replacements.

And they began to return fire.

Their weapons did not spew the same supercharged ions that ours did. They were smaller, less intimidating to look at, but far more precise and deadly. My best buddy in the platoon shrieked and literally melted next to me, his body dissolving into a disgusting, amorphous goo when the beam from an invader's weapon struck him, never mind the phasing body armor he wore.

I took down the alien who got him, but the sight of him dying that way freaked me out more than anything I'd ever seen.

I knew, when my number got called in the selection six months prior, that I was not going to live to see the end of the war. We all did, though we never talked about it, and tried not to think about it. But as we went through our drills, learning how to use our weapons and armor, each of us knew it was futile.

We were all doomed.

Well, maybe not all of us realized it. The Lieutenant, that silly bastard, seemed to really believe we could prevail. So did a few other guys in the unit. But from the get-go, I knew we were on a fool's errand.

So I decided to live it up in the time I had left. Lord knew there were girls aplenty waiting in line to give it up to a soldier, and who was I to deny them their fantasies? It was every man's dream for a while there, and I almost forgot about the fate awaiting me.

Awaiting us all.

I surely never thought it would come for us so soon. Or that we would die such gruesome deaths.

Another buddy getting liquified next to me drew me back to the present, and I hit the dirt behind a fallen tree. Three separate alien beams traced through the air where I'd just been standing, and I breathed a sigh of relief that my reflexes were as quick as they were.

Glancing left and right, I could see two or three other guys from my unit, crouching behind cover as I was. Where was everyone else?

My earbud, tuned to the command circuit, carried the Lieutenant's voice. It sounded like he was beginning to order a withdrawal, but his words turned into an agonized, horrified screech, then all that came through the earbud was static.

The other men on either side of me panicked as the chain of command broke down. One by one, they scrambled backwards, away from the advancing aliens.

And one by one they were struck down, alien beams hitting them the instant they emerged from cover.

It took a minute for me to realize that I was completely alone.

Alien invaders streamed past my position on either side. They apparently didn't realize I was there, and still kicking. For a heartbeat the thought passed through my head that I could make it if I just played dead.

Then a surge of anger, outrage even, filled me.

I can't tell you now why I did it, or how. I don't remember actually deciding to do it, or telling my legs to. Before I even realized it, I found myself standing upright, turning my rifle on alien after alien, incinerating an invader with each shot.

On and on I shot, raking my fire from left to right.

I relished every invader's scream as it went down, every flash of fire as my rounds struck home.

I was going down, but by God, I'd take as many of them with me as I could.

Then the rifle stopped firing. I'd used up the entire ammo receiver. I reached for a replacement, but found my belt pouches empty.

I must have reloaded and fired through them all without realizing it.

All around me, the battlefield was obscured with smoke. Everywhere I looked, all I could see were craters, the shattered remains of alien invaders, and smoke rising from both. There must have been a hundred of the bastards lying dead or mortally wounded in my immediate vicinity.

For a moment, I actually thought I'd won.

Then a gust of wind thinned out the smoke, revealing the massed multitudes of invaders, gathered in a half-circle around me, watching.

Waiting.

I was done.

Fine, if that's how it was going to be, I wasn't going to give the bastards the satisfaction of watching me run.

With a roar, I threw my rifle at the closest of them and drew my bowie knife. Then I charged.

A single invader, armored differently from the others, raised its weapon toward me as I advanced. I knew it would get me before I could do anything with my knife, so I threw the blade at it.

The alien fired as I threw.

It felt like a ball-peen hammer slugged me in the chest, and I fell over. I had only a heartbeat to wonder why I wasn't melting before I lost consciousness.

I couldn't tell you how long I was out, but when I came to, I found myself in a large oval-shaped room.

The walls were painted a light cream color. The ceiling was plain, unadorned except for recessed lighting panels. I was resting on a mattress, or couch, of come sort.

And I was no longer in my body armor. Instead, I wore a loose-fitting grey robe, almost like a hospital gown.

It was hard to move, but I managed to sit up after a few moments of trying. The rest of the room came into view as I did, and my jaw dropped. One side of the room was dominated by a window looking out into space.

I knew it was space, because I could see Luna not far off, and past it, Earth. I'd never been off world before. The view was awe-inspiring, and for a moment, the implication of what I was seeing was lost on me.

"It's quite a view, isn't it?"

The voice surprised me for two reasons. One, I hadn't noticed any other people in the room with me. Two, it spoke perfect english, and in a North American accent.

I looked around for the source of the voice, and beheld a man in his middle years sitting in an armchair not far from me. He had dark brown hair, nearly black, and sharp hazel eyes. His nose was romanesque, and he had large, protruding ears.

I did a double-take.

His ears were not just large, they were huge. And pointed. For that matter, his eyes were not human either: instead of round, his irises were slits, like a cat's.

The alien smirked ever so slightly as I drew back from him. "Believe me, you people look just as strange to us as we do to you."

"How..." I swallowed. "How do you - ?"

"Know your language?" Again, the alien smirked. "If you know the enemy and know yourself, you need not fear the result of a hundred battles."

That phrase seemed familiar somehow, but I couldn't put my finger on it. "I've heard that before," I said, almost to myself.

The alien nodded. "I should hope so. We spent many years training the man you know as Sun Tzu. He never knew it of course."

"You...trained him?" I knew I sounded incredulous. And, well, I was.

"Of course. We make it our business to help the younger species grow, become strong."

This was all coming a bit too fast. Processing what the alien was saying, on top of getting my mind around being alive and on an alien ship was beginning to make my head hurt.

I couldn't find the right words to say, so I settled for shaking my head.

The alien touched something on the arm of his chair, and the wall opposite the window to space flickered, then displayed a series of images. Humans, in all states of dress that obviously spanned history, engaged in battle after battle. The graphic bloodshed made me wince, but the alien only smiled as he watched the stream of images.

"Almost from the beginning, you showed promise. You were strong, resourceful, adaptive. You just needed...prodding...to get you moving down the path to greatness."

More images flashed up on the screen, this time of individuals. Caesar. Genghis Kahn. Sun Tzu. Saladin. Napoleon. Nelson. Kaiser Wilhelm. Hitler. MacArthur. Abu Nadal. Gorshkov. Li Sung. Mendoza. The greatest military leaders in human history streamed past in an unbroken line until, after Thorton, the list abruptly ended.

"We influenced the greatest among you, helped them become better. Without their knowing, of course. And they led you to the height of your strength." He sighed before continuing. "As you can imagine, we were gravely disappointed when you decided to turn away from the path of greatness." The alien shook his head in disapproval.

"No we haven't. We live among the stars now, in peace - "

"Peace!" The alien spat the word like a curse as he turned to give me his full attention again. His features contorted in a grimace of disgust. "Yes, you've lived in peace. And stagnated."

He gestured toward the wall again, where a new image appeared.

This one was video. It only took a second for me to realize I was looking at a live feed from Earth's surface. Bile rose in my stomach as I watched women, children, the elderly, the wounded, and the fearful fleeing before the advancing alien forces.

But they didn't make it far. They fell by the dozen as the aliens fired into the fleeing crowd. There was no audio, but I could imagine their terrified, despairing screams as they sought in vain to escape their fate.

"Look at them," said the alien, contempt in his voice. "Weak. Pathetic. Not one of them has the will to fight for his own survival. Instead, they made themselves sheep for the slaughter." He shook his head again.

"They're unarmed and without training. If - "

"Weapons are nothing. Training is nothing." The

alien tapped the side of his head with his index finger and continued. "Will is everything. The will to not give in. To struggle and overcome, to fight. Show me a coward with training against a person of will who never thought of how to fight, and the willful person will win three times out of four." He leaned toward me, fixing me with his strange gaze. "How many were in your town, and how many of you came out to fight against us? You have more than enough numbers to beat us if you had the will to try. You see the result of your species' cowardice there."

"I don't understand. You *want* us to fight?"

"Of course. Conflict is the driving force behind growth, behind evolution. A species that stops fighting stops improving itself. It stagnates, as you have. We thought that you had grown enough to not need further prodding, but the last several hundred of your years showed us that the maturity to accept the most basic facts of existence still eludes you. And so we have come again, to teach you a lesson you should never have forgotten: to live without conflict is to tread upon the path to oblivion."

I sank back onto the couch, stunned.

The alien's matter-of-fact speech was proof enough that what he said was the truth. All this time, mankind had patted itself on the back for finally finding a way to live at peace with itself, and all the while that very peace was setting us up for extermination.

But if that were so, why...

"Why are you telling me this? For that matter, why am I even alive?"

"Because you have a fighter's spirit." The alien stood and walked over to me. "If your species is to return to greatness, its new leaders must be of the correct temperament. Of all your comrades on the battlefield, only you had the will to fight to the end. That kind of will is exactly what is needed."

I shook my head in denial. "I just got angry."

"And your anger gave you strength." The alien gestured for me to stand up, and I complied, slowly. I was pretty sure I knew what the alien had in mind, but decided to hear him out, anyway.

Rather that speaking, though, he gestured toward the window, and I looked out.

Down on earth, I could see, even from this distance out in space, flashes of explosions in several locations around the globe. They must have detonated some truly massive bombs for us to be able to see them from way out here. We stood there for what seemed a long time, just watching the fireworks.

Finally, the alien spoke again.

"As you can see, if we wished to, we could eliminate your species completely. But we believe you still have promise, so we're giving mankind a fresh start. We will spare a remnant, enough to rebuild in a reasonable amount of time. You will help to lead that remnant on the proper path."

"I'll not be your stooge."

The alien chuckled. "And so you won't. After this is done, you'll never see me or mine again. But we'll be watching, helping, prodding, just as we always have. And hoping that this time, you'll get it right."

"And if I say no?"

The alien was silent for a moment, and I glanced sidelong at him. Rather than looking at me, his gaze remained fixed on Earth. When he finally spoke, his voice carried a hard edge.

"You may refuse, and we'll simply set you back

on Earth. You might even survive to be one of the remnant. But I promise you, life will be less than pleasant. We'll see to that. You'll wish very quickly that you'd accepted our offer."

Turning away from the window, the alien walked back to his chair and touched the arm rest again. Part of the wall near the display screen opened, and a group of people walked in.

They numbered about twenty or thirty, and were all human. Male, female, dark, light, tall, short, slim, muscular, but none fat, they represented all the sub-races of humanity. Leading them was a tall, muscular man with a proud face and hard eyes. It took me a moment to realize where I recognized him from: he was the man in the last transmission from Centauri.

The group stopped when they reached the alien's chair and turned their eyes on me. I felt laid bare, naked, beneath their collective gaze.

"Decide now," said the alien. "Will you join these others as a Lord of the remnant, and lead mankind back to greatness, or will you refuse, and take your chances with those on the world below?"

I looked from the alien to the Centauri man's face, then down the line of humans to the last, a lovely young lady of Czech decent, unless I missed my guess.

Next, I turned and looked out the window, toward the besieged Earth.

It was not a hard decision to make.

MESSAGE FROM THE AUTHOR

Thank you for reading my book. I hope you enjoyed reading it as much as I enjoyed writing it.

Every review helps an author out, so whether you loved this book, hated it, or something in between, please take a minute to tell other readers what you thought. All of the online retailers make it very easy to do, and I would really appreciate it.

Feel free to come say hi at my website or on Facebook. I always enjoy hearing from readers, especially since you all are, collectively, my boss.

I also have a weekly podcast, Story Time With Michael Kingswood, where I read stories and talk through some of the latest goings on in my world. I'd love to see you there.

Thanks again. My best to you and yours.

Warm Regards,
Michael Kingswood

MAILING LIST

If you enjoyed this book and would like word on new releases and special deals from Michael Kingswood, sign up for his newsletter on his website. Guaranteed to be spam-free, you can opt out at any time. And you can rest assured he will not share your information with anyone, for any reason.

https://michaelkingswood.com/newsletter-signup/

SUPPORTING PATRONAGE

Michael would like to invite you to become a supporting member of his website. Similar in concept to Patreon, a few dollars a month will give you access to exclusive content, and help him to focus more of his time to writing fun and exciting stories for your enjoyment.

Sign up at his website:

https://www.michaelkingswood.com/membership/supporting-patronage/

ABOUT THE AUTHOR

Michael Kingswood is 20-year veteran of the US Navy submarine force and a lifelong fan of science fiction and fantasy literature. His work has appeared in numerous collections and anthologies, to include the Fiction River Anthology series from WMG publishing. He holds a bachelors degree in Mechanical Engineering as well as a Master of Engineering Management and a Master of Business Administration. He has four children and currently resides in San Diego.

Find Michael Kingswood online at:

www.michaelkingswood.com

www.facebook.com/michael.kingswood

steemit.com/@michaelkingswood

MORE BOOKS BY MICHAEL KINGSWOOD

Glimmer Vale Chronicles

Glimmer Vale

Out-Dweller

Tollard's Peak

Robbed Blind

Wedding Gifts: A Glimmer Vale Chronicles Story

The Falconer's Stairs

Glimmer Vale Omnibus Edition #1

~

The Pericles Conspiracy

Passing In The Night

The Pericles Conspiracy

~

Dawn Of Enlightenment

Masters Of The Sun

~

Novellas

What Lurks Between

The Necromancer's Lair

The Champion

Veritas Morte

Story Collections

Tales Of Adventure #1

Tales Of Adventure #2

Short Story 10-Pack

A Jar Of Mixed Treats

Short Fiction

Michael has also published a number of shorter works,
links to which can be found on his website.